Dear Parents,

   Psalty in Alaska deals with the fear of failure. When we don't try new things because we are afraid of failing, we cannot learn and grow. But as long as we do our best, that's all God expects of us. In the following pages, Psalty the Singing Songbook shows us that sometimes God uses failure to teach us how to succeed.

   As with all Psalty products, for this new adventure story, we've chosen struggles and concepts that affect everyone trying to live their Christian faith. We believe that if you learn these concepts as a child, they will stay with you throughout your adult years. And you will be better equipped to live a joyous life, committed to Christ.

   Now snuggle close to your little one and follow Psalty; his booklet Rhythm, and their trusty dog Blooper on a challenging adventure in Alaska.

Ernie Rettino and Debby Kerner Rettino

PSALTY IN ALASKA

Copyright © 1991 by Ernie Rettino and Debby Kerner Rettino.

Scripture quotations are from the *International Children's Bible, New Century Version*. Copyright © 1983, 1986, 1988 by Word Publishing.

Library of Congress Cataloging-in-Publication Data

Rettino, Ernie, 1949-
    Psalty in Alaska / Ernie Rettino and Debby Kerner Rettino ; design
and illustration by Dale Wehlacz.
      p.   cm.
    "Word kids!"
    Summary : Rhythm's experience in a dogsled race in Alaska shows
him that God does not expect you to win every time, as long as you
do your best.
    ISBN 0-8499-0893-0
    [1. Sled dog racing—Fiction. 2. Alaska—Fiction. 3. Christian
life—Fiction. 4. Books—Fiction.] I. Rettino, Debby Kerner,
1951- . II. Wehlacz, Dale, 1960- ill. III. Title.
PZ7.R32553Po   1991
[E]—dc20

                              91-498
                                CIP
                                    AC

Printed in the United States of America

1 2 3 4 9 RRD 9 8 7 6 5 4 3 2 1

PSALTY in ALASKA

Characters and Story by
Ernie Rettino and Debby Kerner Rettino

Design and Illustration by
Dale Wehlacz

WORD *Kids!*

WORD PUBLISHING
Dallas·London·Vancouver·Melbourne

"Okay! Okay! Calm down Blooper!" said Psalty. The songbook and his blue and white dog were going to meet Rhythm. The booklet was on his way home from school. Blooper saw Rhythm a block away and charged toward him.

Jumping on his best buddy, Blooper licked Rhythm's face all over.

"Whoa, Blooper, I'm glad to see you, too!" said Rhythm. The little booklet felt like he needed a friend today.

"Hi, Rhythm," said Psalty. "How'd school go?"

"Hi, Dad. It was okay, I guess."

"How did band tryouts go?" Psalty asked.

"I didn't try out," said Rhythm with a heavy sigh.

"Why not, Rhythm? You are such a good drummer!" Psalty's voice was full of concern.

"Maybe I'm not," said Rhythm. The little booklet's binding drooped with sadness.

Psalty tried to think of just the right thing to say. "Rhythm, it sounds like you're afraid of trying because you might not make it."

"You're right. What if I didn't get it? The other kids would laugh at me." Rhythm felt awful.

"God won't laugh," said Psalty. "He just wants us to do the best we can."

"But if I can't be the best, I don't want to try at all," Rhythm insisted.

"Son," said Psalty kindly. "Being best is nice, but everybody can't be best. God gives each of us different talents and abilities. We'll be better at some things than others. But we don't have to be afraid of trying."

"I don't get it," said Rhythm. "Why not?"

"Messing up doesn't make you a loser," said Psalty. "Failing doesn't make you a failure. You're just learning what to do right the next time."

"I think I get the idea," said Rhythm.

"Trying helps you figure out what you ARE good at," assured Psalty. "Give yourself a chance."

Just then Psalty and Rhythm passed a travel agency. In the window was a poster.

COME TO ALASKA!

Experience The Great Outdoors!

FACE NEW CHALLENGES!

"Rhythm, would you like to come with me to Alaska?" asked Psalty.

"For real?" asked Rhythm. "Can Blooper come?"

"Sure! Let's check out the great outdoors and face new challenges together!" said Psalty.

Psalty and Rhythm bought their tickets and said
good-bye to Psaltina, Harmony, and Melody.
Soon they were on a jet bound for Alaska!
As the plane landed, Rhythm was
tingling with excitement.
Alaska! . . . Land of gold rushes,
mountain men, polar bears! Wow!

Psalty and Rhythm walked through the streets with Blooper beside them. They met miners who were trading gold nuggets for cash. "Come pan for gold with us," the miners offered. "It's a challenge to live in the wild."

They saw fishermen selling their catch. "Come fish with us . . . it's a real challenge in a storm!"

A lady wearing a coonskin cap called out, "Last call to sign up for the dogsled race."

"A dogsled race?" Rhythm asked, as Blooper's ears perked up. "That sounds like fun! But, what if we don't win?"

"Rhythm," Psalty answered, "let's enter the race. This is a challenge to face, whether we win or not."

Blooper barked in agreement. "You can be the lead dog, Blooper," Psalty promised. "What do we have to do?" Psalty asked the lady.

"Sign your names right here, and get your gear together. The race is tomorrow," the lady informed them. "All the racers are staying at the Frontier Lodge. We're having a big party for the racers tonight. See you there!"

Psalty, Rhythm, and Blooper got busy getting ready for the race. They bought a sled, food, snow gear, and a dog team. Blooper stuck his chest out as he nosed the other dogs hello. He wanted them to know he was the lead dog!

That night Psalty and Rhythm met the other racers at the party.

"Howdy, I'm Big Ed," said a tall, rough-looking man.
"You up from the Lower 48*?" he asked.

"Yes, we are, I'm Psalty, and this is my booklet, Rhythm.
Is this your first race?"

"Oh no!" Big Ed laughed. "It's my fifth race. But I always
come in second. I'm gonna win this time."

"Well, may the best man . . . er . . . uh . . . book win."

The next morning Psalty and Rhythm were at the starting line eager to go. Blooper couldn't wait! "On your marks, get set, . . ." BANG! The gun went off and the race began.

Psalty and Rhythm quickly pulled into the lead.

"Good dog, Blooper!" Rhythm called out. Big Ed
was close behind in second place. On and on the race
went. Sleds and dogs were taking curves and corners at a
dizzying speed. Blooper loved the feel of the wind in his
face!

As dusk fell, the skies clouded over, and it began to snow. It snowed, and it snowed and it snowed even harder. They were in the middle of a blizzard*! "Which way do we go, Dad?" Rhythm asked.

"I don't know. I can't see the course," answered Psalty with alarm.

The snow was so thick they could hardly see each other. "I think we're lost," said Psalty. "We're going to have to stop until the storm is over."

"Look, Dad, an igloo*," Rhythm said. "Maybe we can stay there."

Inside the igloo was an Eskimo named Inuk. "Come in out of the storm," he invited. "Bring your dogs in, too."

"Thank you," said Psalty and Rhythm gratefully. They all piled into the igloo and warmed up around the fire. Poor Blooper! His paws were blue with cold!

"Have some squaw candy*," offered their host.

"Candy?" asked Rhythm. "Yum!" He bit into the pink strip Inuk gave him. "This isn't candy, it's dried fish!" said Rhythm with surprise.

The Eskimo laughed. Rhythm actually liked squaw candy!

Psalty and Rhythm were very tired. They thanked God for the warm igloo to protect them in the blizzard. Then they snuggled up with the dogs and fell fast asleep.

The next day the blizzard was gone, but so were the markers for the race! "What do we do, Dad?" Rhythm asked.

"We'll have to use our compass to find the way,"
answered Psalty. "Which way is north, Rhythm?"

Rhythm checked the compass. "That-a-way!"

They thanked their Eskimo friend and sped off over the
snow. Along the way they passed lots of wild animals.

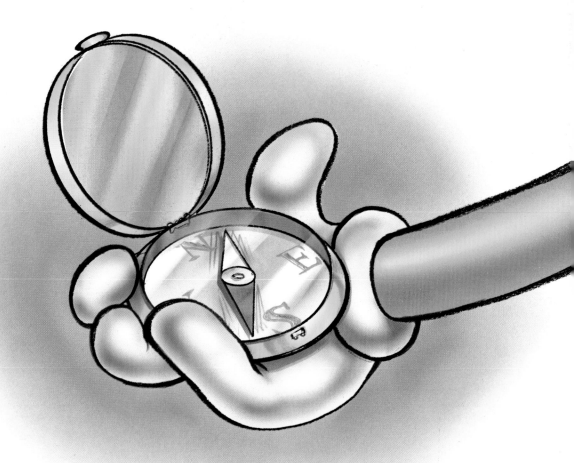

They saw seals, moose, and even polar bears. One polar bear ran beside them for a while, but he finally waved good-bye.

"We haven't seen any of the other racers, Dad." Rhythm was getting worried.

"We must be ahead of everyone else," Psalty answered smugly.

"Dad! That cliff isn't on the course! I checked the map. We've been going the wrong way!" Rhythm exclaimed. "I must have read the compass upside down!"

"Uh-oh, now what are we going to do?" asked Psalty.

"We'll just turn around and go the right way," decided Rhythm. "We've come too far to give up now."

"That's my booklet!" said Psalty.

Rhythm and Psalty quickly turned the sled around. Blooper and the dog team ran fast to make up lost time.

Over the next hill they saw another dog team.

"Come on, Blooper, go faster!" shouted Rhythm.

The dogs ran as hard as they could. Soon, they passed the other sled!

Then, just ahead was Big Ed! Psalty and Rhythm could
see the finish line and hear the cheering crowd.

Blooper found a last bit of extra power and almost
passed Big Ed. But Big Ed saw them coming and went even
faster. Try as they might, Psalty and Rhythm couldn't catch
up. Big Ed raced across the finish line first. Psalty and
Rhythm were just behind him, in second place.

The crowd was cheering wildly. Psaltina, Harmony, and Melody had come to see the race. They ran over to hug Psalty and Rhythm. They gave Blooper a big hug, too.

"Congratulations, Big Ed. You kept trying and you deserved to win!" said Psalty and Rhythm.

"Thanks. But you ran a very close race," answered Big Ed.

"I'm glad we entered the race," said Rhythm. "Even though we didn't win, we did our best, and that's all God expects. I don't have to be afraid of failing. Trying things is how I learn and grow. Can we enter the race again next year, Dad?"

"Sure thing, Rhythm!" agreed Psalty.

Psalty and his family flew back home, and Rhythm went back to school. Now Rhythm was eager to try out for band. He wasn't afraid of failing. He knew all God expected was for him to do his very best. Psalty was very proud of him.

GLOSSARY

Lower 48 —   A term used to mean all the States except Alaska and Hawaii.

Blizzard (bliz´-ərd) —   A Storm with strong winds and heavy snow.

Igloo (ig´-l$\overline{oo}$) —   A small round Eskimo house usually built of blocks of hard snow or sod grass roots. The round shape and thick snow blocks keep out the cold.

Squaw candy (skwô kan´-d$\overline{e}$) —   Strips of dried fish.

THERE'S MORE TO COME! Follow Psalty and family's round-the-world adventures in these other great stories:

PSALTY IN THE SOVIET CIRCUS—a memorized Bible verse brings Psalty comfort when he is mistakenly thrown in jail.

PSALTY IN THE SOUTH PACIFIC—being marooned on a South Seas island shows Harmony how trouble can help us grow.

PSALTY ON SAFARI—an exciting game-show win and a trip to Africa show Melody that helping with God's work can be more exciting than spending money on herself.

PSALTY IN EGYPT—a kidnapping in the shadow of the Great Pyramid ends in a lesson about the life-changing power of prayer and God's love.

PSALTY IN AUSTRALIA—a vacation "down under" gives Psalty's family a glimpse of God's amazing creativity and reminds them that God has a unique plan for everyone.